This book belongs to

_____

the sweetest, kindest, smartest, bravest,
fastest, toughest, greatest kid that ever was.

my name is not ALEXANDER

story by Jennifer Fosberry • pictures by Mike Litwin

For Luke Frescoln:
Dare to dream!
Jennifer Fosberry

sourcebooks
jabberwocky

Published by Sourcebooks Jabberwocky, an imprint of Sourcebooks, Inc.
P.O. Box 4410, Naperville, Illinois 60567-4410
(630) 961-3900
Fax: (630) 961-2168
www.jabberwockykids.com

Library of Congress Cataloging-in-Publication data is on file with the publisher.

Source of Production: Oceanic Graphic Printing, Kowloon, Hong Kong, China
Date of Production: January 2011
Run Number: 14070
Ages 4 and up

Printed and bound in China.
OGP 10 9 8 7 6 5 4 3 2 1

For Poppi, Bars, and
Googi—the boys that
play in my life. **—JF**

For Caiden and
Carter. **—ML**

"Good morning, ALEXANDER," the father said. "It's time for breakfast, and then let's play ball."

"*My name is not Alexander!*" said the little boy.

"Then who has been sleeping in my son's bed?" asked the father.

"I am **THEODORE**, the greatest, grandest president who ever was!"

"Well, Theodore, **PARK** yourself here and **SAVE** your **ENERGY** for today's game."

"Theodore, finish eating and get ready to go," the father said.

"My name is not Theodore!" said the little boy.

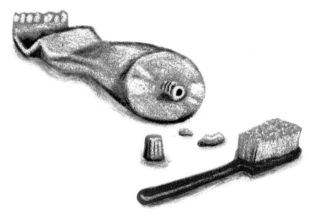

"Then who is going to brush his teeth?" asked the father.

"I am **THOMAS**, the greatest, brightest inventor who ever was!"

"Well, Thomas, let me see that **BRILLIANT** smile **LIGHT** up the room."

"Let's go, Thomas," the father said.
"We don't want to miss the big game."

"My name is not Thomas!"
said the little boy.

"Then who will
help me load the car?"
asked the father.

"I am **JOSEPH**, the greatest, proudest warrior who ever was!"

"Well, **CHIEF**, let's make a **PACT** not to be late."

"Okay, Joseph," the father said.
"Let's go see Grandma."

"My name is not Joseph!" said the little boy.

"Then who is going to bring in this beautiful bouquet?" asked the father.

"I am **FRED**, the greatest, smoothest

"Well, Fred, **GLIDE** on in there and give your partner a **WHIRL**."

dancer who ever was!"

"Dinner's over, Fred,"
the father said. "I need your help."

"My name is not Fred!"
said the little boy.

"Then who's going to
help me with the dishes?"
asked the father.

"I am *Jackie*, the greatest, bravest ball player who ever was!"

"Well, Jackie, you **stole** my heart, now clear **home plate**."

"Pj's on Jackie,"
the father said.
"It's almost time
for our campout."

"My name is not Jackie!"
said the little boy.

"Then who's going to
help me pitch the tent?"
asked the father.

"I am DADDY, the greatest, coolest father who ever was!"

"Well, Daddy, give me a HIGH FIVE and get those pj's on."

"Tent time, Daddy," the father said.
"Bring your sleeping bag."

"My name is not Daddy!"
said the little boy.

"Then who's going to
sleep under the stars
with me tonight?"
asked the father.

"It's me, **ALEXANDER**, the coolest, bravest, smoothest, proudest, brightest, grandest, greatest boy that ever was," said the little boy as he fell asleep and dreamed about who he would be...

...**TOMORROW.**

MEN WHO CHANGED THE WORLD

THEODORE "TEDDY" ROOSEVELT (1858–1919):

Teddy Roosevelt was born in New York City to a wealthy family. As a boy Teddy was often sick. With his father's help, he worked to improve his body by doing exercises and playing sports. He put all his effort and enthusiasm into everything he did. As an adult he had many government jobs, including police commissioner. He often walked dangerous streets to meet police officers and the people they protected to learn what needed to be done to keep everyone safe. During the Spanish-American War he raised a volunteer group of fighters known as the "Rough Riders." He led this brave group in an attack straight up San Juan Hill and became famous for his leadership and daring. Teddy was eventually elected vice president to President William McKinley. When McKinley was assassinated, Teddy became the 26th president of the United States. As president he worked hard to save beautiful natural areas of the United States as open parks for everyone to enjoy. Teddy loved to hunt and be outdoors. One of his most famous hunting trips was in Mississippi. He was unable to shoot anything, so his guides tied an old bear to a tree to give him an easy shot. Teddy thought this was awful and refused. The event was all over the news and a toy maker made a stuffed toy bear in his honor. "Teddy" Bears have been favorite toys of children ever since.

A **PRESIDENT** is a person elected to lead the country.

THOMAS ALVA EDISON (1847–1931)

Thomas Alva Edison was a famous inventor. He was a curious kid and his experiments often got him into trouble. One time he accidently set his father's barn on fire. His teacher did not think he was very smart because he did not pay attention in class and he asked so many questions. His mother took him out of school and taught him at home. Thomas eventually worked at a telegraph company before he started his own company to make devices. He built a large lab and was called "the Wizard" of Menlo Park, New Jersey. His lab tried more than 3,000 kinds of materials before using baked carbon thread to make the very first light bulb. Thomas invented many things besides the light bulb, including the phonograph (record player), the first movie camera and projector, a cement mixer, a copying machine, and a battery. He holds a record number of 1,093 patents for his inventions. After Thomas died, everyone turned off their lights (including the Statue of Liberty) on the night of his funeral to honor his most famous invention.

An **INVENTOR** is a person who comes up with ideas for new things and then tries to make them work.

CHIEF JOSEPH (1840–1904):

Chief Joseph was the leader of the Nez Percé Native American tribe of Northwest Oregon. The U.S. government wanted the tribe to leave their home in the Wallowa Valley and move to a small reservation in Idaho. The Nez Percé did not want to leave, but Chief Joseph thought it would be better than to fight with the powerful U.S. Army. But some of the younger tribesmen were angry at the government and joined a raid that killed several U.S. soldiers. Chief Joseph knew this would be seen as an act of war and decided to escape to Canada with his tribe. For over four months they traveled about 1,600 miles with the U.S. Army in pursuit They were finally trapped during the Battle of Bear Paw, only 40 miles from the Canadian border. After five days in the bitter cold and the loss of many warriors, Chief Joseph negotiated with the army to let his people return home and surrendered with a famous speech. He said, "I am tired; my heart is sick and sad. From where the sun now stands, I will fight no more forever." The government sent the Nez Percé to reservations in Kansas and Oklahoma. Many died before the tribe was finally allowed to return to the Wallowa Valley ten years later. Chief Joseph remained the leader of his people and spoke about the unjust treatment of Native Americans and how he hoped for free and equal treatment. He died in September 1904, still in exile from his homeland. His doctor said he died of a broken heart.

A **WARRIOR** is a person who shows strength and courage during battle.